Plop City

A humorous story
in a familiar setting

First published in 2006 by
Franklin Watts
338 Euston Road
London
NW1 3BH

Franklin Watts Australia
Hachette Children's Books
Level 17/207 Kent Street
Sydney
NSW 2000

A CIP catalogue record for this book is available
from the British Library.

ISBN 0 7496 6561 0 (hbk)
ISBN 0 7496 6569 6 (pbk)

Series Editor: Jackie Hamley
Series Advisors: Dr Barrie Wade, Dr Hilary Minns
Design: Peter Scoulding

Printed in China

FOR BILLY, TOM, WILLIAM AND QUINNLYN – E.R.

Plop City

Written by
Enid Richemont

Illustrated by
Gwyneth Williamson

W
FRANKLIN WATTS
LONDON•SYDNEY

Enid Richemont

"I love surprises, but I'd rather have them popping up in my garden than plopping on to my head!"

Gwyneth Williamson

"Birds plop lots of seeds around my garden, which is lovely! But a seagull plopped on me once and it was more fishy than flowery. Everyone said it was lucky!"

Fat strawberries grew in the mayor's back garden. Juicy raspberries, blueberries and apples grew there, too.

Prize roses grew in the mayor's back garden. Daisies, sunflowers and poppies grew there, too.

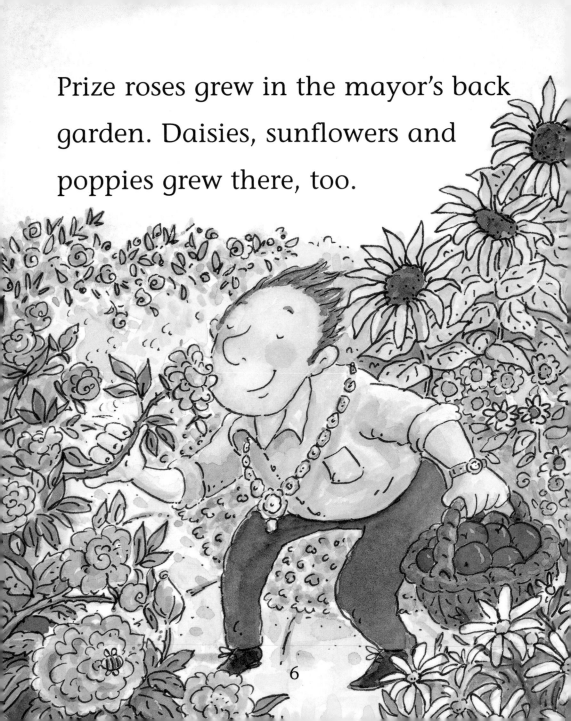

Birds loved to land in the mayor's back garden – starlings and pigeons, thrushes and blackbirds.

They pecked at the strawberries.

They gobbled up the raspberries.

They swallowed the blueberries
and made holes in the apples.

They pecked off pink rosebuds
and daisy heads.

They tried poppies, sunflowers
and marigolds, too.

9

The mayor's gardeners yelled: "Shoo!"

But the birds took no notice.

They put up scarecrows, but
the birds weren't scared off.

11

Then the gardeners ran around with
pop guns – pop, POP, POP!
At last, the birds rose up and
flew away.

POP

POP

They flew over the streets.

They flew over the city.

By then they had eaten so much

that they all wanted to poo.

Yellow sunflower poo fell PLOP!

on to the army parade ground.

14

Pink rose poo fell PLOP!
on to a rich lady's hat.

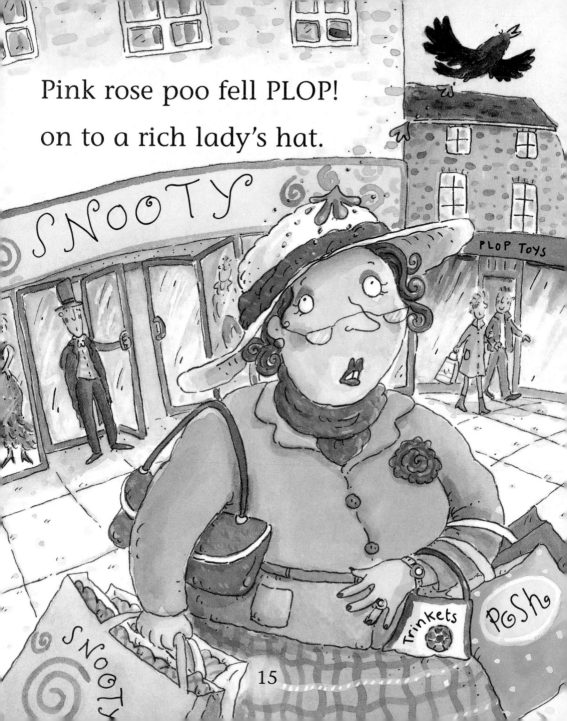

15

Red strawberry poo went PLOP!

on to a police car's windscreen.

Blueberry poo went PLOP!
on to a little dog's nose.

Poppy poo fell PLOP! all round
Gran's back yard.

And apple poo streaked
across the mayor's best suit.

The soldiers hosed down the army parade ground.

The rich lady threw out her poo-stained hat.

SUPERMARKET ← ENTRANCE

The policeman washed down his windscreen in the station car park.

The mayor wiped down his jacket,
and dropped the cloth.

Gran shook her head and sighed.

"Just look at all that bird poo!"

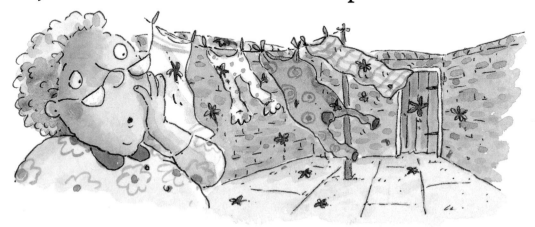

But the little dog just sneezed

– A-TISHOO! A-TISHOO!

Weeks went by. Sometimes the sun shone, and sometimes it rained.

The seeds inside the bird poo began to swell – sunflower seeds and rose seeds, tulip seeds and blueberry seeds and strawberry seeds, too.

One day, sunflowers began growing
in the army parade ground.

Strawberries sprouted in the
police station car park.

Soon a little apple shoot pushed
up outside the Town Hall ...

... and blueberries started growing
in the park on the hill.

A rose shoot popped up round
the back of the supermarket ...

... and Gran goggled at all
the poppies in her back yard.

Then the birds returned to the mayor's back garden. The gardeners ran out with pop guns. Pop, POP, POP!

The birds rose up and flew over the
city. Plop, PLOP, PLOP!

Notes for parents and teachers

READING CORNER has been structured to provide maximum support for new readers. The stories may be used by adults for sharing with young children. Primarily, however, the stories are designed for newly independent readers, whether they are reading these books in bed at night, or in the reading corner at school or in the library.

Starting to read alone can be a daunting prospect. READING CORNER helps by providing visual support and repeating words and phrases, while making reading enjoyable. These books will develop confidence in the new reader, and encourage a love of reading that will last a lifetime!

If you are reading this book with a child, here are a few tips:

1. Make reading fun! Choose a time to read when you and the child are relaxed and have time to share the story.

2. Encourage children to reread the story, and to retell the story in their own words, using the illustrations to remind them what has happened.

3. Give praise! Remember that small mistakes need not always be corrected.

READING CORNER covers three grades of early reading ability, with three levels at each grade. Each level has a certain number of words per story, indicated by the number of bars on the spine of the book, to allow you to choose the right book for a young reader:

GRADE 1	GRADE 2	GRADE 3
50 words	130 words	250 words
70 words	160 words	350 words
100 words	200 words	450 words